Romani and Traveling people throughout the world have a long history. Their culture is based around their language, and their love of story, music and animals. Their tales are passed on from generation to generation, often by word of mouth alone. Despite many challenging times, Travelers have survived and thrived, ready to share their stories with everyone.

Many Travelers do not live in a house on a street, but in homes on wheels instead. They do not go to work in the same building day after day. The woods and fields are their workshops. They make beautiful things, often from recycled objects that others have thrown away, and they trade goods wherever they stop their caravans.

Travelers are hard-working. Wherever they may be, they find a way to turn their talents and efforts into food, clothing and whatever else they need to keep them rolling from place to place.

Yokki and the Parno Gry is a tale that celebrates the power of storytelling and creativity within the Traveler community.

*To my family
and all the traditional Traveler storytellers – past, present and future*

Richard

To my family

Katharine

✳ ❀ ✳

First published in 2016 by Child's Play (International) Ltd
Ashworth Road, Bridgemead, Swindon SN5 7YD, UK

Published in USA by Child's Play Inc
250 Minot Avenue, Auburn, Maine 04210

Distributed in Australia by Child's Play Australia Pty Ltd
Unit 10/20 Narabang Way, Belrose, Sydney, NSW 2085

ISBN 978-1-84643-927-8
CLP030517CPL06179278

Printed and bound in Shenzhen, China

3 5 7 9 10 8 6 4 2

A catalogue record of this book
is available from the British Library

www.childs-play.com

✳ ❀ ✳

Glossary:

Parno Gry: *White horse* - **Phuri Dai:** *Grandma* - **Daddo:** *Daddy* - **Chavvies:** *Children*
Folki: *People* - **Chopping horses:** *Selling/swapping horses* - **Tel te Jib:** *Hold your tongue*

YOKKI

and the

PARNO GRY

RICHARD O'NEILL • KATHARINE QUARMBY

illustrated by MARIEKE NELISSEN

There was once a Traveler boy called Yokki.
He lived with his large family in canvas tents.

Yokki's grandfather Elijah loved buying and selling horses
more than anything else. His grandma, the Phuri Dai,
was skilled at selling, and respected for her wisdom.

There was no work to be had in early spring, so the whole family made things to sell. Yokki's sister Serafina made the most beautiful paper flowers, and Yokki carved fine wooden spoons.

"Time for us to move on," Yokki's Daddo would say,
when spring turned into summer.

"Let's get packed up, Chavvies," Mother would smile,
excited to be moving again and following the old trading ways.

Everywhere they stopped, Yokki's father mended
pots and pans, and sharpened tools and knives.

Yokki loved to sell the spoons he had made. It gave him
the chance to talk to all sorts of people, Traveling Folki
and settled folk, and to listen to their stories.

In the late summer and fall,
the family picked fruit and vegetables
for local farmers, saving money
for the winter when work was scarce.

The family would gather around the fire every night to tell stories. Everyone agreed that Yokki told the best tales. He would retell the stories that he had heard from other people, mixing them up and adding bits of his own.

Every year, they all looked forward to the horse fairs and other festivals. Serafina would swap her flowers for jewelry. Grandfather Elijah would buy and sell horses, 'chopping' them for a good price.

Best of all, the Phuri Dai would
lead them in the dancing each night.

One year the summer was wet and the harvest was poor. Many of the crops just rotted in the ground. Even Farmer Tom had no work for them.

"Sorry, but since we got these new machines I don't need so many extra hands," he said. "Perhaps next year, if you learn to drive?"

"We needed that money," said Father. "How will we survive the winter without it?"

"Let's move on," suggested Grandfather.
"There will be some work or trade in the next town."

But when they reached their usual camping ground they found it had been fenced off. Father looked grimly at Grandfather and Grandmother. "We can't stop here."

The Phuri Dai nodded. "We'll have to go on.
It's not much, but I know a place of old where we can stop."

The family finally set up camp late that night on a tiny patch
of wasteland. They built a blazing fire and Yokki decided
to tell a story from his dreams to cheer everyone up.
He told of a Parno Gry, a powerful white horse
who would fly into camp and take
him away.

"When I am on the Parno Gry I can see lands where fruit hangs heavy on the trees. There's plenty of work harvesting, and everyone can eat their fill." Huddled in their blankets, everyone felt the warmth of the sun on their skin and forgot their hunger.

The patch of wasteland was bare and scruffy,
but the family had nowhere else to go. For a while
Yokki's stories about the wonderful Parno Gry made them
forget their troubles, but their lives got harder and harder
as winter approached, and it was difficult to stay cheerful.

The next day brought another disaster.

"Bessie's limping," Serafina panted. "She's gone lame."

This was bad news. Bessie was their best horse.
"I'll take her to Farmer Tom," said Father.
"He'll look after her for the price of her food.
He's a good man."

Every day of trading brought new disappointments.
Hardly anyone wanted to buy their crafts.

At the market, Aunty struggled to get a good price for the hens.
"That's only half what they're worth," she cried,
as someone tried to bargain with her.
But she knew half was better than nothing.

Grandfather Elijah had to sell the old goat, Nancy,
and the carts. Father got a bad deal on the donkey.
"I'm so sorry," he said.

All they would have left were their tents,
their two dogs, and Bessie, once she was better.

The next night, as the family huddled together,
Yokki's youngest cousin Mary pulled at his sleeve.
"Take us far away. Tell us another story about the Parno Gry,"
she pleaded.

Grandfather Elijah grew angry. "You are filling their heads
with dreams of a made-up future," he shouted. "Tel te Jib!"

The Phuri Dai told him to sit down.
"Sometimes, dear ones, all we have are our dreams," she said.
"They keep us going until the next opportunity appears.
Tonight, all we have is Yokki's story. Let's enjoy it."

"In my dream the Parno Gry came and we all climbed on its back. It soared beyond the clouds to a fine land. As we flew low we saw a bustling market, with folki like us, selling strong handmade furniture, and a great crowd of people buying their goods."

With this hopeful image in their minds, everyone forgot their troubles and fell into a happy sleep.

A cry woke the family.

Yokki was shouting.
"It's come! It's the Parno Gry!"

Everyone ran outside. In front
of them stood a huge white horse
with steam coming out of its nostrils.

Just as Yokki had dreamed, the Parno Gry flattened itself
to the ground. The family hastily packed their tents and
the few belongings they had left. All of them, along with
their dogs, climbed onto the Parno Gry's powerful back.

Running faster and faster,
the Parno Gry soared up into the night sky.

The adults were afraid, but the children looked down
in wonder as the cold, dark land disappeared below them.

After a while, the Parno Gry landed again.

The air was cold, but trees and rocks provided shelter, and a stream ran gently through a clearing. Some large fallen trees meant there would be plenty of firewood. There would be enough left over to make furniture too.

"Let's get the tents up," said Yokki's father.

"Chavvies, take a look around!" Grandfather called.
"See what else this land can provide."

"Look, look!" Jentina had come across a wild garden,
with apples still hanging on the overgrown trees.

"Over here!" Absolom had dug into the fine, crumbly soil,
to find it full of buried treasure! Potatoes!

That evening they lit a fire and danced for joy.
They cooked the first good meal in a long time
and the delicious scent filled the air.

The Parno Gry came over to Yokki.
It was time for it to go.
"We cannot thank
you enough,"
Yokki said.

He stroked the animal.
"You have shown us
a new and exciting future."

Yokki whispered a final farewell.

Then they all waved goodbye
as the Parno Gry rose up, and out of sight.

To this day, generations of Yokki's family believe that as long as they value children's imaginations, the Parno Gry will inspire them with new ideas and possibilities – even in their darkest hours, just when they need them most.